The Dinosaur Dig

By Veronica Wasserman

Based on the television series *Franny's Feet*
created by Cathy Moss and Susin Nielsen

GROSSET & DUNLAP

GROSSET & DUNLAP
Published by the Penguin Group
Penguin Group (USA) Inc., 375 Hudson Street, New York, New York 10014, USA
Penguin Group (Canada), 90 Eglinton Avenue East, Suite 700, Toronto, Ontario M4P 2Y3, Canada
(a division of Pearson Penguin Canada Inc.)
Penguin Books Ltd., 80 Strand, London WC2R ORL, England
Penguin Group Ireland, 25 St. Stephen's Green, Dublin 2, Ireland
(a division of Penguin Books Ltd.)
Penguin Group (Australia), 250 Camberwell Road, Camberwell, Victoria 3124, Australia
(a division of Pearson Australia Group Pty. Ltd.)
Penguin Books India Pvt. Ltd., 11 Community Centre, Panchsheel Park, New Delhi-110 017, India
Penguin Group (NZ), 67 Apollo Drive, Rosedale, North Shore 0745, Auckland, New Zealand
(a division of Pearson New Zealand Ltd.)
Penguin Books (South Africa) (Pty.) Ltd., 24 Sturdee Avenue,
Rosebank, Johannesburg 2196, South Africa

Penguin Books Ltd, Registered Offices:
80 Strand, London WC2R ORL, England

© 2008 DECODE Entertainment Inc. Franny's Feet is a trademark of DECODE Entertainment Inc.
All Rights Reserved. www.frannysfeet.com. A Decode production in association with Thirteen/WNET New York.
The PBS KIDS logo is a registered trademark of the Public Broadcasting Service and is used with permission.
All rights reserved. Used under license by Penguin Young Readers Group. Printed in the U.S.A.

Library of Congress Control Number: 2007016556

ISBN 978-0-448-44710-0   10 9 8 7 6 5 4 3 2 1

Franny Fantootsie loves to go to her grandfather's shoe repair shop. She always meets new people and goes on *frantastic* adventures.

"Grandpa, come see what I made!" Franny called as she placed the final card on top of her house of cards.

"I'll be right there," Grandpa said.

"Hurry, Grandpa. It's delicate!" Franny said.

"I'm coming, Franny! I just need to find something first," Grandpa called back.

Just then, the bell on the shop door rang and a man walked inside.

"A customer!" Franny cried.

"And what can we do for you?" Grandpa asked the man.

"These work boots are taking a sick day," the man joked. "Look at the size of this hole in the sole!"

"Don't worry. I'll have them back on the job on Monday," Grandpa promised.

"Could you put these in the fix-it box, please?" Grandpa asked Franny. "Sure, Grandpa!" she said.

Franny climbed down from her stool and carried the boots over to the fix-it box.

Giggling, she put on the boots and smiled. "Where will my feet take me today?" Franny wondered, and in a flash of stars, she was whisked to a faraway place.

Franny found herself in the middle of
a dusty desert. People with tools and
shovels were working everywhere.
   "Where am I?" she asked.
   "You're in the badlands," a young
boy who was standing nearby said.
"But don't worry, there's nothing bad
about them. It's just a name."
   Franny giggled. "That's good," she
said.

"I'm Joey," the boy said. "And this is Rex. And that's my mom over there," Joey continued, pointing to a woman digging.

"I'm Franny. It's nice to meet you," Franny said as she scratched Rex behind the ears. "Why is everybody digging?"

"They're digging for fossils," Joey answered.

"What are fossils?" Franny asked.

"They're what's left of things that lived millions of years ago," Joey said.

"Today," Joey said, "we're looking for *big* fossils. We're looking for dinosaur bones!"

"Wow!" Franny said. "I'd love to find a dinosaur. Can I help?"

"Sure!" Joey said.

Franny and Joey were busy digging when Rex let out a bark.

"What is it, Rex?" Joey asked.

"Maybe he found a dinosaur!" Franny said.

"Maybe it's a brontosaurus," said Joey. "Or—"

"Or a gopher," Franny said as a gopher popped out of the hole. The gopher grabbed Joey's shovel and ducked back into his hole. "Hey! Give that back!" Joey yelled.

Franny grabbed for the shovel, and the gopher ducked back into the hole again. "Galloping gophers! This is silly," she said.

"Let's watch Rex," Joey said to Franny. Rex was sniffing the ground. Joey and Franny followed. Rex stopped at one of the holes, and the gopher popped back up.

"Gotcha!" Franny said as she grabbed the shovel.

"Good boy, Rex!" Joey said as he patted Rex's head. "He's the best tracking dog ever."

"Hey!" Franny said. "If Rex can sniff out a gopher underground, maybe he can track down dinosaur bones, too!"

"It's worth a try," Joey said. He pulled a dinosaur book out of his backpack.

"See this, Rex? These are dinosaur bones," Joey continued. "Let's go find some."

"I think he got the idea!" Franny said as Rex started running away.

"Thatta boy, Rex! Find the fossils!" Joey said as he and Franny chased after him.

Then Rex came to a stop. "Did he find something?" Franny asked.

"Yeah," Joey said. "Our lunch."

"Well, we did work up an appetite," Franny said, giggling.

"Let's break for lunch," Joey said.

"Okay," Franny said. "Let's sit down over there on that rock."

"Do you like peanut butter and banana sandwiches?" Joey asked.

"Do I ever!" Franny answered.

"We'll save the cookies for later," Joey said.

"I can't believe we haven't found any dinosaur bones yet," Franny said, taking a bite out of her sandwich.

"Sometimes my mom digs for weeks and doesn't find anything," Joey explained.

"Weeks?" Franny cried. "But I only borrowed these boots for today!"

"Then I guess we better look twice as hard this afternoon."

Then Rex grabbed the bag of cookies on the ground next to Joey and started to run away.

"Rex! Those are for all of us!" Joey yelled.

"Come back here, you cookie bandit!" Franny cried as she and Joey chased after Rex. Soon they found themselves on top of a hill.

Suddenly, Joey stopped.

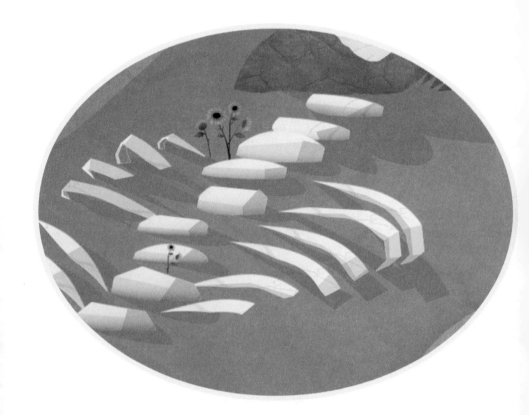

"Franny, look!" Joey cried, pointing down to where they had been eating their lunch. "We weren't sitting on a rock—"

"We were sitting on a dinosaur!" Franny said.

"We've got to show my mom!" Joey said.

"Good work, kids! This is a wonderful discovery!" Joey's mom said.

"I can't believe it was here all along," Joey said.

"Sometimes," Joey's mom said, "the hardest things to see are right under your nose."

    With that, Franny realized it was time for her to go. She still had to show Grandpa her house of cards. "Good-bye, everybody!" she said. "I had a *frantastic* time with you!"

    "Thanks for all your help, Franny," Joey said.

    "Bye, Franny!" Joey's mom said.

Franny landed back in her Grandpa's shop. "That was dino-rific!" she exclaimed.

Franny jumped out of the boots and started to put them into the fix-it box. "What's this?" she asked as something fell out of one of the boots.

"It's a fossil!" Franny said. "Now I have another treasure for my shoe box."

Franny was excited to show Grandpa her house of cards. But when she returned to the table, she saw that he was still looking for something at his workbench.

"Grandpa, what are you looking for?" Franny asked.

"My glasses," he said. "I know you have something to show me and I won't be able to see it without them."

Franny looked at Grandpa. "You mean *those* glasses?" she asked, pointing to the top of his head.

Grandpa looked surprised as he pulled his glasses off his head. "They were up here all along? Now I feel silly," he said.

"Don't feel bad," Franny said. "Joey didn't."

"Joey?" Grandpa asked. "Who's Joey?"

Franny told Grandpa all about Joey and Rex and Joey's mom and how they had found the dinosaur bones. "It goes to show, sometimes the hardest things to find are right under your nose," she said.

"Or on top of your head," Grandpa joked.

"Come on, Grandpa. Come see what I made!" Franny said as she led him over to her house of cards.

"Ah, will you look at that!" he said. "You made a house of cards and it's still standing! Now that's something to see!"

Franny went on a wonderful adventure today, and another one is just around the corner. "Where will my feet take me tomorrow?"